AF409488

Savior In The Sand

By

Jonathan A. Miller

Chapter ONE

"Mind your own business," Hector Hilde muttered. "Or what?!" the belligerent man shouted. He started to invade his personal space, forcing Hector to step back. "Can you please just leave me alone, I really don't want any trouble," Hector said, trying to de-escalate the situation.

"He's just intoxicated," he thought to himself. The bartender just stood and watched as the drunk man was slowly backing Hector into a corner.

Something snapped inside Hector. His fight-or-flight instinct kicked in and he pushed the man away, attempting to create space. The drunk man took this as a threat and swung at Hector, hitting him square in the teeth. He paused for a second, then shook it off.

His practices that he had learned from the streets as a child began to kick in. Hector threw a couple of lower body shots to attempt to open up the his guard, then threw a strong cross to the man's jaw, rapidly spinning his head and knocking him out.

The adrenaline was surging hardcore. Hector stared down at the man, who was still unconscious. "Watch who you fuck with next time, will ya?" he said furiously as he turned away and walked out of the bar. Everyone in the bar had stopped what they were doing and stood in silence.

One stranger walked over to the drunk man and gave his face a little slap. "Wakey wakey." he said with a slight smirk on his face, then proceeded to walk back to his table.

The drunk man's eyelids slowly opened up. He was still very delirious yet. He let out a shocked gasp, coming to the realization that he was just unconscious. "Whyda-fukanwhadu hell," he mumbled under his own rapid breaths. He looked around furiously and confused. The drunk man then stumbled over to the bathroom and slammed the door behind him.

Hector slammed the car door shut in frustration. He laid his head into his hands upon the steering wheel. *"It was just self defense,"* Hector thought to himself. *"The man was clearly drunk and didn't know what the hell he was doing. Shit happens."* He turned the key in the ignition and drove himself back home.

When he entered his apartment, Hector made his way to the bathroom to wash up his face. He looked in the mirror and saw the blood streaming from the open cut on his lip. All of his teeth seemed fine, but the lip was definitely going to need time to heal.

Once he was finished up in the bathroom, Hector made his way to the living room. He saw the leftover pizza that he had ordered the night before. He didn't really feel like cooking tonight, so he ate the leftovers. He then turned on the TV and sat there for a while, still thinking about everything that had happened tonight.

Chapter TWO

The next morning, Hector got up and decided he wasn't going to eat breakfast today. He carelessly slipped on his clothes and drove to work. He still had a major cut on his lip from the night before. All of his coworkers seemed concerned and asked him what had happened.

His excuse was that he had tripped and busted his lip on the corner of the concrete stairs that led to his apartment. It seemed like a believable story to himself, but he could tell that no one else was buying it.

The night had fallen and everything seemed still. It was a slow and painful day at work for Hector, but he somehow managed to push through. Dragging his feet as he walked and thinking too much about what had happened. He would try to tell himself to let the thought go, but just couldn't.

As he was walking back to his silver car, he noticed something out of the corner of his eye. A dark figure of what looked to be a woman wearing a hoodie slipped behind the wall of the brick building. He looked away and then rapidly looked back, realizing that something was off. "What the fuck was that?" he said out loud.

With a sense of curiosity, he took his phone out of his pocket and turned the flashlight on, shining it in the general direction of where he saw the figure. Hector slowly walked over to the brick wall.

"Hello?" he shouted into the darkness. "Are you okay?" He turned the corner of the wall and shined his flashlight down the alleyway. There was nothing.

Nothing but a dumpster sitting at the end with bags of trash flowing out. Hector let out a sigh of relief. "Probably just seeing things," he told himself. He turned away and slowly walked back to his car.

Hector shut the car door and rapidly shook his head a little in attempt to wake himself up. He decided to just ignore what had happened and turn on the radio. As he pulled out of the parking lot, he heard a faint banging sound. It seemed constant and fairly distant, like it was coming from the building he had just left. "Nobody should be here," he said to himself. "Everybody has gone home already."

The banging sound continued and started to irritate Hector a little. He sensed that something wasn't right. A slight chill ran up his spine and all the hairs on the back of his neck stood up, dwelling on the thought that something might be lurking around. He was extremely curious, however.

Hector put the car in park and hopped out. He frantically looked around the area to see if anyone was watching him. Realizing that nobody was around, he decided to investigate the sound.

As he approached the building, the banging grew louder. Listening closely, he soon realized the metallic nature of this sound. Almost like the sound of sheet metal being dented.

Hector walked back to the alleyway where he thought he had seen someone earlier, and noticed a ladder to the left of the dumpster that led to the roof. He began to climb this ladder, hoping that it was stable enough to support his weight. As soon as he reached the top, the sound suddenly stopped.

He quickly whipped out his phone and shined the flashlight around. Peering around into the vastness of the empty roof, Hector saw nothing out of the ordinary. He decided to continue investigating however, slowing walking around and attempting to locate someone or something. He located a small metal trapdoor that seemed to head inside the building.

As Hector shined his flashlight at it, he noticed that it was severely dented and stained with a deep black substance. "What the hell?" he whispered. He reached out and touched the substance with his fingertips. It felt dry yet very viscous. It stained his fingers and he was unable to wipe it off.

"Aw, you've gotta be kidding me." Hector said with disgust. He kept wiping his fingers on his shirt, but nothing. He even spat on the substance, but that had no effect whatsoever. Hector had no clue what he had just touched, but it definitely did not seem to be a normal liquid. He ignored it and continued to search around.

There was another metal trapdoor located not too far from the first one. It was also very dented and had more of that odd black substance dripped into a puddle on the top. Hector decided to use his empty small metal pill case that was attached to his keychain to scoop up some of the liquid. He popped the lid back on and shoved it in his pocket.

As he continued towards the opposite side of the roof, he stumbled into something unusual. The same girl that he had seen earlier was standing in the corner of two brick walls adjacent to the rooftop entrance. She was facing away, wearing torn up dark red skinny jeans, white sneakers that were falling apart, and a black hoodie with the hood pulled up over her hair. It was hard for Hector to tell, but she looked to be about in her twenties.

He didn't really know what to do or how to handle the situation. "Hello?" he said politely to the girl. "Are you lost?" he asked.

No response. Hector stepped a bit closer. He waved his arms as if she had eyes in the back of her head. "Are you awake? You're not supposed to be up here. You could get into some serious trouble," he explained.

Something about that triggered the girl to move. She began walking towards an open ledge of the building, hiding her face behind the hoodie. She then turned and faced the ledge, holding her arms wide out like she was about to drop. There was muffled crying coming from behind her hood. "No!" Hector shouted "Don't do it, it's not worth it!"

He ran towards her, but it was already too late. She leaned forward and let herself drop. Hector made it to the ledge and peered over into the concrete parking lot below. There was nothing there. Not even a body.

Chapter THREE

Hector laid on his bed, staring at the ceiling of his apartment. He was losing sleep over what had just happened a couple hours ago. None of it made sense to him.

It was around three o'clock in the morning and Hector still hadn't got any sleep. He was frustrated. He tossed and turned as his thoughts raced. Eventually, he decided to get up and grab a drink of water.

He made his way over to the sink and filled a glass full of tap water. He then walked over to the TV in the living room and decided to watch some cartoons.

As he sat down on the couch, something out of the corner of his eye caught his attention. A dark-haired woman's grinning face peered through the kitchen window at him. By the time he looked over, it was already gone. Hector jumped backwards on the couch as he spilled the glass of water all over himself.

"Hello?!" he shouted at window in fear. "Who is that?!" There wasn't any response whatsoever. Hector stood up and grabbed the wooden baseball bat that was hung up on his wall for decoration. It was very heavy, so it could definitely pack quite the punch.

Hector walked over to the kitchen window and peered outside. *Nobody.* Just the alleyway and the convenience store next to him. He dropped his guard and set the baseball bat down. "Am I going crazy?" he thought to himself with his hands pressed up into his hair.

His heart was still racing. He definitely felt like he saw something. Hector checked some of the other windows and locked his front door, just in case. "Maybe I'm just sleep deprived," he told himself. He ignored the whole situation and changed his clothes, which were now soaked in water.

Surprisingly, Hector was eventually able to fall asleep. However, he had to keep many of his lights on and lock the bedroom door in order to feel safe.

It was around two in the afternoon when Hector woke up. He didn't have work today, so he was able to finally sleep in. He decided that he was going to go hang out at the boardwalk, which was about forty-five minutes away from where he lived.

Hector hopped into his silver sedan, and began driving. It was quite freeing for him to go on a little road trip after working so much. He made sure not to speed like he usually did. The route he took to the boardwalk was packed with highway patrol officers that could easily catch him in the act.

After a long drive, he finally made it. He walked up to the sign that said:

*"Welcome to **Valbeach Boardwalk**"*

Hector only came here every once in a while when he wasn't so busy. It was like his little getaway spot. It was sunny out today, so it seemed like a perfect opportunity. He walked down the steps onto the beach.

It was nice. There were people playing volleyball and goofing around, while others sipped on bottles of beer and chatted. Hector decided to see if he could join in on the volleyball. He walked up to one of the individuals.

The man was wearing a blue short sleeved t-shirt and tan cargo pants. His hair was long and reached down his back. "Hey!" Hector shouted with a friendly wave. "Can I join in?" he said as he approached the man. He smiled and gestured towards Hector. "Sure, why the hell not!" he said in response.

He hung out with the group for a bit and even got their information to hang out in the future. "It's getting late, I gotta head home before it gets too dark," Hector said to the group. "Same here, we probably don't want to stay on this beach after eleven o'clock hits," one of the gentleman said.

"What do mean by that?" Hector asked with concern. The man laughed. "Oh, nobody ever told you about *The Missing Lifeguard?*" he said to Hector. "Oh come on Nate, this bullshit story again?" one of the other gentlemen said. "What? She's real," he responded. "What are you guys talking about?" Hector asked.

Nate let out a little chuckle. "The Lost Lifeguard is an evil spirit that roams the beach after hours," he explained. "Rumour has it, people have been drawn into the water at nighttime by an attractive female spirit and disappeared underneath completely, nowhere to be found."

"So kind of like a Siren from Greek Mythology," Hector said. "Sort of, but no crazy pirate ships," Nate responded. Hector had his doubts. They were probably just trying to spook him. "Well, I won't believe it until I see it," he said. Nate giggled a bit. "Hey, at least it would be quite the sight before you die!" Nate said through his laughter.

"Anyways, you take care. It was nice meeting you," Nate said to Hector. "Thanks, we'll have to hang out again sometime. And maybe we'll dare to stay after eleven," he said with a grin. Nate chuckled as he walked off with his group of friends.

Hector got his phone out of his pocket and took a few selfies of himself on the beach, just for fun. "Time to head home," he said to himself as the darkness of night surrounded him. He made his way back to his car and fired up the ignition.

His headlights flicked on, revealing a figure down the alleyway ahead of him. It was tall and menacing looking, the way it stood with its back to Hector and its fists clenched.

Hector jumped back in his seat. "What the hell?" he said quietly to himself as he squinted at the figure. It looked to be a man wearing a denim jacket and brown cargo pants. His black hair was slicked back and tattoos ran down his left hand. Hector looked at little closer.

He was holding something in his left hand. Something shiny. Hector stepped out of his car to confront the individual. "Hey," he shouted. "You alright?"

The man slowly turned around to face Hector. *"This was a bad idea,"* he thought to himself. *"I should just leave."* As the man fully turned around, Hector's car headlights suddenly shut off. It was now pitch black and he could no longer see the stranger.

Hector panicked and jumped back into his car, locking the door behind him. He took a deep breath and flicked the headlights back on. The man was gone and something lied where he was once standing.

It was the shiny object he was holding. Hector badly wanted to leave right now, but his curiosity got the best of him. Slowly, he opened his car door again and stepped out. His headlights kept the alleyway lit up perfectly.

Hector began walking over to the shiny object. Once he got close enough, he then realised what it was. It was a gold picture frame with a photo inside. Hector walked up to the photo and picked it up. He looked closely.

It was a group picture of him and his family. *"What is this doing out here?"* he thought to himself. *"And why was this stranger holding it?"*

As he was thinking, something darted past the front of his car, casting a quick shadow on the walls for a split second. Hector whipped around. "Who's there?!" he said out loud, feeling extremely unsafe now.

Hector wasn't going to stick around to find out. He ran back to his car with the photo in hand, locking the door once again.

He shifted into reverse and booked it out of the parking lot.

When Hector got home, he sat on his bed and took a deep breath. He lifted up the picture and looked closer at it. There was his mother, father, brother, and.. someone else. Whoever it was, they were scribbled out.

He then remembered when this photo was taken and who was there with him. The crossed out person was his sister. *"Why?"* he thought. *"Who would hate her that much to cross her out?"*

Something didn't seem right. However, Hector was getting tired and he needed to get some rest. He put the photograph to the side for now and lied down, trying not to think about it too much.

Chapter FOUR

The sun shined through the bathroom window as Hector opened up the cabinet and pulled out his electric toothbrush. He began brushing. He looked at himself in the mirror and smiled. "Still handsome as ever," he said to himself.

Once he was finished with that, Hector ate his breakfast and got ready to head out for work. He slipped on his jacket, grabbed his keys, and headed out for the day.

After what he had seen on the roof the other night, work just didn't feel the same. Not to mention, the encounter he had last night was still fresh in his mind. Hector wanted to tell his co-workers, but he felt like somebody would snitch, then he would get into trouble for venturing around on the roof after hours. So, Hector decided to keep the story a secret.

The job he worked at was in a package handling facility. He received packages, then sent out others onto trucks. It wasn't the most interesting job, but it paid the bills. At least he had his co-worker friends there to mess around with to make the day go by a bit faster. As long as he didn't get himself into trouble with the managers again.

Hector slid his worker identification card into the device and punched out for lunch. There were a couple of different fast food establishments nearby that he always got his lunch from. He walked outside to make his way down the street to "Keryl's Fried Chicken," his favourite place to buy lunch.

On his way out of the facility, Hector looked over towards where that girl had dropped the other night. He was still baffled yet extremely unsettled about the whole scenario. He walked back over to the spot to look for any other marks or hints of an impact.

There was a dried puddle on the pavement which Hector assumed was just water, as it had rained a couple of nights ago.

He reached down and slid his fingers across the wet surface. It felt.. warm. He peered down at his fingertips and noticed that they were now dark red.

Hector fell backwards onto the pavement. "What in the.." he said in shock. His fingertips were now covered in what looked like fresh blood. He got up and ran back inside to the nearest bathroom and slammed the door behind him, ignoring his confused co-workers.

The warm water washed away most of the blood, but there was still a slight red hue stained onto his fingertips. Not all of it was gone, but it was good enough. His shower at home would probably wash it off with time.

He stepped out of the bathroom to see two of his co-workers staring at him with both hands in their pockets. "Are you okay Hector?" one of them asked. "Yeah.. I.. I'm alright. Just a nose bleed," he said in a shaky voice as he looked down at his fingertips.

"Oh okay. We were just worried when we seen you book it to the bathroom at high speed," the other co-worker said with a chuckle. Hector laughed nervously with them. "Yeah, it.. it's all good. No need to worry about me," he responded to them. However they noticed the unusual nervousness in Hector's voice and didn't seem to really believe him.

"Are you sure you're okay? You just seem a little bit shaken by something," one of them said. Hector paused for a bit, running through his thoughts.

If he showed them the puddle, the cops would probably be called in an instant and an investigation would have to be started. The security cameras would have already caught him climbing onto the roof, so he could totally get caught for trespassing. However, it would feel right if he reported the suicide he witnessed, that way they could figure out what actually happened. He had no choice.

"Follow me," Hector said as he waved his hand. The workers look at each other, confused. He led them outside to the wet spot. Hector pulled out a used tissue from his pocket and dabbled it onto the spot.

He lifted it up and showed his co-workers the blood soaked tissue. They both froze in place. "Oh, that's probably not good," one of them said. "It's probably just an animal's blood," said the other. He had a great point. It could just be the blood from a killed animal, but it just didn't make any sense. Why would it be right at the spot in which the girl had dropped?

Hector was still too afraid to actually tell them what he had witnessed the other night. His co-workers would for sure snitch on him for climbing on the roof and he would lose his job. So, he decided to keep his mouth shut.

"I wouldn't worry about it Hector. It's probably just from a dead animal," one of them said to him. "You're right," he said, not mentioning anything about what he had previously witnessed. "Go enjoy your lunch and really wash those hands again, just to be safe," the other co-worker responded. And so, Hector kept quiet about it and ate his lunch at the restaurant.

Chapter FIVE

Hector was getting ready to head home for the night. He was still thinking about that puddle of blood and how it was coincidentally placed under the spot where the girl dropped. It didn't seem right.

It was the dead of night and once again, Hector was one of the last to leave the facility. The entire place sat in silence and stillness. He wanted to check something. Hector walked to that same corner where he had first spotted the girl.

He shined his phone's flashlight around, scanning for evidence or anything that she might've left behind. Hector approached the ladder. Something was smeared onto the metal bars, so he looked closer.

What he saw sent chills down his spine. Bloodied hand-prints. Each one grasping the ladder as they ascended their way up. He could see each palm indentation from the grip.

"Were these that same girl's hand-prints? I don't remember these being here the first time I climbed up," he thought to himself.

Hector hesitated for a moment, then shoved his phone back in his pocket. The alleyway plunged back into darkness. He used his jacket sleeves as gloves to make his way up the ladder, so he wouldn't have to touch any blood.

As he neared the top of the ladder, he felt something clasp around his right ankle. He tried to pull up and away, but it was stuck. He tried to look down and see what he was stuck on, but it was way too dark to see anything.

"Shit," Hector grunted in frustration. The grasp was quite strong, yet felt cold and wet. He removed his right hand from the ladder and reached into his pocket for his phone.

As he did however, the phone slipped out of his hands and fell. He heard it smack onto the pavement below. "God-dammit!" he shouted. His ankle was still caught on something and he couldn't even see what it was.

Hector reached his hand down carefully to his right ankle to see if he could removed whatever had him stuck. His hand stumbled upon the object. It felt sort like.. a bag or.. maybe a hand? He felt it out a little more and realised that it was indeed a hand. Soft, cold and wet.

Hector freaked out and lost his grip on the ladder. His body flipped backwards, smashing his head against the ladder. His vision blurred as he darted his eyes around. Agonising pain surged through the back of his skull.

Something was still holding him by the ankle as he hung upside down. Hector reached his hands up and attempted to pull himself back upward. He eventually succeeded, however blood was now trickling from the back of his head and he still felt that cold hand wrapped around his ankle.

He looked down to find out what was holding him, however it was too dark to see. Hector screamed and wriggled his right leg around, trying to break free, but the grip was monstrous. "Get the fuck off me!" he screamed at the mysterious hand.

And it seemed to listen to him. The grip finally broke free and Hector scrambled up the ladder as fast as he could. He reached the rooftop and scrambled as far from the ladder as he could. He laid on his back, attempting to catch his breath.

Blood was still oozing from Hector's head. Adrenaline seemed to be numbing most of the pain, but not for long. He stood up and looked around for another way down. There was no way he was going back to that ladder.

Hector spotted something on the roof. *A hatch.* He walked over to it and gave it a tug. It was locked. He kicked the hatch, denting it in. "Damn-it!" he shouted. The only way down was that ladder.

Rolling up his pant leg, Hector touched his ankle and felt something wet. It was hard to tell, but it looked like blood. He wasn't sure it was his though, because there was no wound at all. Whatever grabbed him must have been injured.

He ignored the blood and continued searching the roof for an alternate exit. But there was nothing. Suddenly, sirens started blaring in the distance. Hector assumed it was probably just an ambulance or something.

Two police cars rounded the corner of the street with their lights on. They seemed to be heading for the entrance of the facility. If he got caught here past hours, he would get into some serious trouble. Possibly even a trespassing charge along with getting fired.

He wasn't going to stick around to find out. Hector made his way back to the ladder that he was grabbed on. He peered down the ladder into the darkness. He had no choice. Grabbing the cold metal of the ladder, Hector made his way down slowly.

Nothing was grabbing him this time, but he definitely had to move faster. Car doors slammed in the distance and faint voices could be heard. Hector descended the ladder quickly. He eventually got to the bottom, but it was pitch black. His phone was no longer there either.

Feeling his way through the darkness, Hector eventually got to the corner of the wall at the back of the building. He peered around the corner where there was plenty of light and seen two officers with flashlights making their way to the back of the building.

He quickly whipped his head back into cover, hoping they didn't see him. But one of them began shouting, "Hey!" in his direction. Hector acted fast and ran to a fence adjacent to the wall he was behind. He climbed his way up.

"Who's back there?" one of the officers shouted. Hector reached the top and flopped over, hitting the ground with a roll. He got up and darted into the woods just as a flashlight was pointed in his direction. He sprinted through the dimly moonlit forest, hoping they weren't chasing.

There was small stream ahead. It looked to be knee deep, but Hector couldn't really tell in the dark of the forest. He didn't care though. Adrenaline was surging through his veins, so he jumped right in.

The water only reached the middle part of his shins, but the current was strong. He continued through, till eventually the water creeped up to his waist. Then eventually his chest.

The current was way too strong, and the stream was only getting deeper. Dogs barked in the distance and voices echoed throughout the forest, but before Hector could check his surroundings, he was swept off his feet in an instant.

He couldn't breathe. It was dark and he felt the painful impacts every time he slammed into a rock or branch. This so called "stream" was more like the rapids of a river.

He kept kicking and flailing his arms, attempting to get a gasp of air every chance he got. Eventually, his shirt got caught on something and stopped him.

Chapter SIX

Hector surfaced and gasped for air, as he hung there from a branch by his shirt. He looked around, vision still blurry. Something suddenly caught his attention. A flash of light directly across from him. He looked closer and could barely make out a figure.

It was *that girl.* The same one he saw a couple nights ago. She was now sitting there on a rock next to the stream, with her legs crossed and her hood up. Her head was facing down, so he still couldn't make out a face.

A bell sounded throughout the forest. *Ding.. Ding.. Ding..* then a pause. *Ding.. Ding.. Ding..* It continued. I was as if someone was walking with a cow bell, but Hector couldn't quite make out where it was coming from.

The girl was still sitting there. She was only about twelve feet from him, just staring downward. However, when Hector looked at her once again, the unexpected happened. Her gaze met his, and what Hector saw shocked him. An ear-to-ear grin with no teeth. Eyes that glowed white with no pupils.

Her nose appeared to be missing and there was a deep scar across her entire face. Hector's heart began to race. He was still hanging from the branch, freezing in the water. The bells continued to echo throughout the forest.

Suddenly, the girl started speaking in a raspy voice. *"He's coming,"* she said in a fearful tone. Hector was shocked that she just spoke. "Who's coming?" he asked the girl.

"The.. red man," she replied, still sounding torn and raspy. Hector was absolutely confused. "What are you talking about? And who are y-" but before he could finish, the girl stood up and bolted off into the forest.

Hector sat there for a moment, baffled. Either way, he needed to get himself unstuck. He grabbed onto the branch and was able to barely pull himself on top.

Luckily, the branch held his weight just fine. He crawled his way off the branch and made it to the edge of the stream.

Hector sighed. He checked himself over to assess the damage. Cuts and bruises were everywhere. Blood also dripped from his brow and into his eye.

He finally got himself together and stood up, looking around rapidly to see if anyone was watching him. The bells were still echoing in the forest. They now sounded they were moving. Like someone was walking around with a bunch of different bells. As he looked around, nothing caught his attention, but he felt like he was being watched.

Hector decided he needed to get out of this forest, so he started following the stream back up. He would rather return to the police than witness whatever was in this forest.

It didn't seem right. Who was that girl? And what was wrong with her face? And who is the *red man* she was referring to?

Hector put it to the side for now and focused on what he needed to do. He continued up the stream, but the bells sounded closer than before. He started walking faster.

But it only grew louder. So he broke out into a light jog. Louder, and louder. Until it sounded like it was right behind him. Hector began running so fast, he nearly tripped several times.

A loud grunting and heavy breathing began to pick up behind him. Someone or something was definitely chasing him now. It was now life or death for Hector. He pushed on as hard as he could, adrenaline surging through his veins.

Up ahead was a walking trail that led away from the stream. He had no clue where this would take him, but Hector had no other choice. He sprinted down the path, still hearing the grunting and bells right behind him. Whatever was chasing him made not a footstep, but it was definitely right on him.

Straight ahead a couple dozen feet down the path was a small building and a sign above that read, *"Restrooms."* Hector booked it towards the entrance of the men's room. He whipped the door open and slammed it behind him, quickly checking for a lock.

But there wasn't one. It was a public restroom with nothing but a few stalls and a urinal. He ran into one of the stalls in the corner and locked the door behind him.

Hector jumped up onto the toilet seat in an attempt to hide his feet. But it was now quiet. No bells, no grunting. Hector sighed in relief.

Slam! All of a sudden the main door to the bathrooms swung open. The grunting started again. Bells ringing as whatever it was silently moved throughout the restrooms. Hector quieted his breath instinctively.

A faint red glow moved around the restrooms. It stopped at the first stall. Heavy grunting and bells echoing in against the walls.

Squeak. The first stall's door swung open slowly. The glow then moved to the second stall. *Squeak.* That door swung open. His stall was the last one. However, Hector had a plan.

The red glow stopped at his stall door. He noticed something odd. Something was dripping where the glow was. A dark substance. Maybe blood?

Thump. It pushed against the locked stall door. A loud frustrated grunt sounded from the other side. *Thump!* Harder this time. It was going to break the door down. Hector had to act.

He silently hopped off the toilet seat and crawled over to where the stalls divided. A loud crash along with the sound of the broken metal lock clinked against the tiles.

Hector rolled underneath the divider and into the other stall at the same instant the door crashed open. He then looked up through the open door of the stall he was in. He caught a glimpse of something dark moving into the stall Hector was just in.

A figure of some sort. But it was weird, there was nothing connecting it to the ground. As if it's legs faded into nothingness. And of course there was that red glow shining on the floor like a spotlight.

There wasn't time to think over what he just saw. Hector made a run for it. He booked it as fast as he could out the main door of the restrooms and darted off into the forest.

As he did, an angry deep yell could be heard from the bathroom and it did not sound human. Fear flooded over Hector. His legs began to feel weak and he could barely breathe.

He stopped for a second to catch his breath and whipped his head around to look behind him. The main door to the restrooms swung open. And before he could make out what the figure was, a whisper sounded out from directly in front of him.

Hector whipped his head back around to face that girl again. She was just standing there, staring straight at him with those empty white eyes and a toothless grin. *"I told you,"* she whispered.

The sound of angry grunting and bells ringing were closing in on Hector. A tear came to his eye. "Please.. please," he sobbed. "Can you make it stop?"

Hector looked down, flooded with tears. The girl stepped right in front of him and placed a hand on his shoulder. He looked right up into her eyes. But something was different.

The face was now.. human. A familiar face. Then, it flooded over Hector. "Oh my god.. Emma? Is that.. you?" he said through tears. She smiled in response. A normal smile. A familiar smile.

"I missed you," she replied. Hector smiled back. "I missed you too.. sis," he responded. She reached in and gave Hector a firm hug. He did not want to let go. Not like he did in the past. Hector closed his eyes. The memories flashed by.

What he saw that night on the roof of the building at work, when that girl jumped, that was what his sister had done at a hotel roof in Miami. He tried to stop her the same way he did at his workplace a couple days ago.

"Where have you been sis? I thought you were gone," Hector said. He finally opened his eyes. *She was gone.*

The red man was gone as well. Hector was left alone in the middle of the woods, cut up and bruised. He dropped to his knees, head in his hands and began sobbing again. There was no getting her back.

Chapter SEVEN

Hector woke up, surrounded by doctors. "He's awake," one of them said to another. "Okay, we need to get his side of the story," a male voice called out. Hector peered around the room.

In the corner sat a sheriff. "Hey son," he said with a slight southern accent as he chewed his gum. He then pulled out a pen and notepad. "Mind tellin' me what happened out there?" the sheriff asked. "We found you unconscious lying in a field by the Hamden hiking trail," he continued.

Hector hesitated. "I.. I don't really remember," he answered. The sheriff sighed and rolled his eyes. "Well, you gotta 'member something, right? How ya got there, what you were doing?" he asked.

"I'm.. I'm having trouble-" Hector said as a nurse cut him off. "He's probably got a concussion. Look at his head," the nurse said as she pointed at his forehead. The room sat in silence for a moment.

The sheriff let out another sigh and stood up. "Well, if he remembers anything, let me know. I had my men out there searchin' for hours after that disturbance call," he said. "Will do," a nurse replied. The sheriff shut the door behind him as radio chatter echoed in the halls.

Hours passed and Hector was finally being released from the hospital. The doctors said there were no brain injuries or anything serious, so they put him on painkillers and released him. As far as the police situation went, there wasn't enough proof for anything against Hector so they just let it slip.

As soon as Hector got home, he flopped onto his bed and stared at the ceiling for a while, thinking about his sister. He didn't want to tell the sheriff anything because he knew they would think he was crazy. How had he seen her that night? Was he going crazy or did that actually happen?

Hector didn't have any answers. "I need

to get sleep," he told himself. And so he did. Yet he was having dreams of nothing but, what happened last night. The red man chasing him, his sister hugging him. What did it all mean. Did the red man symbolise something in correlation to his sister's death?

Tap Tap Tap. Hector woke to the sound of something tapping on his bedroom window. He reached over and flicked on his bedside lamp. The light illuminated the room enough so Hector could barely see the closed blinds of the window.

The sound began again. *Tap Tap Tap,* in a slow rhythm. He stood up out of his bed, staring at the blinds. Was someone on the other side? Hector slowly made his way over as the tapping continued. He finally reached the window. Slowly and carefully, he opened the blinds.

It was her. His sister again. Staring through the window with tears in her eyes. "Emma," Hector gasped. He was so excited to see her face again. He flipped the locks on the window and pulled it open.

In an instant, she looked back up at Hector with a look of distress and released her grip from the windowsill, vanishing below with not a sound.

Hector dropped to his knees. "What is happening," he sobbed to himself. Suddenly, his cell phone began to ring. Hector rushed over to see the name on the phone. *Emma.* He immediately picked it up.

"Sis.. please come back," Hector cried through the phone. There was a long pause. *"I miss you too,"* she replied. *"But the red man is the only thing in our way,"* she continued. *Beep.* The call dropped.

What was she talking about. Who is this red man and what does he have to do with anything? Hector sighed and set his phone down on the nightstand. He needed answers.

Hector picked his phone back up and looked at his recent calls. His sister's old number was there. He tapped on her name and began ringing the number. It took a while, but someone did eventually answer. A faint breathing could be heard.

"Hello?" Hector muttered. "Sis, are you there," he continued. Nothing but heavy breathing came through. "I need answers!" Hector shouted. "Please. I tried to save you."

She finally started speaking. *"C.. D.. I.."*

she whispered. "What?" Hector asked. *"C.. D.. I.."* she repeated, only louder and more stern. "What is that supposed the mea-" he asked, but she hung up once again. Hector threw his phone on the carpet in frustration and sat on his bed.

"C. D. I." he repeated to himself. Were they somebody's initials? Or a place? Hector got up and walked over to his laptop and flipped it open, powering it on. He opened up his browser and put in those letters. "C. D. I."

Most results didn't seem to have any correlation. Energy companies, medical facilities, etc. But there was one result that stood out to Hector. *Charles Dahlman Inn,* located in Miami, where his sister took her life. Was that it? Wasn't that the same hotel she jumped from?

Hector opened the location on maps and zoomed into a street view. *That was it.* He remembered it so clearly. Firefighters, police and paramedics stood in this same spot that night with the flashing lights of their vehicles. Hector slammed his laptop shut. He needed to go there.. *right now.*

Chapter EIGHT

The ignition cranked, firing up the car. Hector input the address for the hotel into his GPS. It was a three hour drive, but he had to do it. He needed answers.

Down the road he went, making sure not to make any wrong turns or get himself lost. Seconds passed. Then minutes, then hours. Until Hector eventually made it to Miami. It was truly a beautiful place, even at night.

Drunk college kids chatting on the sidewalks, having the time of their lives. There was occasionally the poor man begging for change. Going up to car windows that were stopped at red lights, trying to get your attention.

Hector was focused, however. He had one objective in mind. That hotel. And before he knew it, there it was. Right before his very own eyes. *"Charles Dahlman Inn,"* the sign read.

He pulled up to the entrance and flagged down the valet. "Name please," the brown haired clean looking valet asked. "Hector Hilde," he responded. "I'm not on your list, but I'd like to make reservations," Hector continued. The valet paused for a moment.

"Sure thing," he said. "Head inside and our front desk staff will get you all set up. Would you like me to park your car for you, good sir?" the valet asked. "Yes please," Hector responded. "I would appreciate that greatly." And so, he went inside as the valet carefully drove his car to the parking garage.

Hector spoke with the front desk staff and got himself the highest floor available. It definitely wasn't cheap, but he needed the answers. He rode the elevator up to floor twenty-five, where his room was located.

Key card in hand, Hector swiped the door open and dropped his bags inside. He was going to wait until tomorrow night, which just so happened to be the fifth of August, exactly five years from when his sister passed. It had to mean something. That this would all be lining up the way it did.

Hector slid the soft and silky sheets over his head and finally got the rest that he needed. Before he knew it, the sun rose over the horizon, peering through the unsheathed windows.

Knock knock. "Room service," a woman's voice called out from the other side of the hotel room door. "Yeah, come in," Hector said with a groggy voice.

The locked beeped and the door slowly swung open as a young lady with blonde hair a green polo and khakis walked inside. "I'm just going to vacuum and take some of your dirty towels if that's okay," she asked. "Yeah, go ahead," Hector responded.

As the lady cleaned his room, something caught his attention. A stain on the carpet. Purple glitter nail polish. Exactly what his sister used. *"Did she have this same room when she stayed here?"* Hector thought to himself. He looked at his key card with the room number. *"157,"* it read.

Hector couldn't quite remember if that

was it, but it seemed likely, being that it was near the roof and there was what looked like her nail polish on the carpet. He put it to the side for now.

"I'm going to head out for the day," he told the cleaning lady. "Ah, where you heading to? Anywhere fun?" she asked. Hector smiled. "The beach of course," he replied. She smiled back at him with beautiful blue eyes. She was surprisingly pretty.

"Well, have fun! And catch me something from the ocean," she said jokingly. Hector blushed a little and let out a chuckle. "I'll find something, don't worry," he said. "As long as it doesn't sting or bite me."

They both laughed together for a moment and waved at each other as they parted ways. Hector figured it was okay to relax for a little bit before he did what he came here for.

He started up his car and drove out of the parking garage towards the beach, blasting his favourite song, "Take me to the beach," by Imagine Dragons. He pulled up to the parking lot and paid for his spot at the booth.

Hector hopped out of his car, grabbed his towel and walked barefoot into the soothing hot sand. Eventually, he reached his spot and threw his towel down, ready to absorb the warm embracing rays of the sun.

He laid there for a while, still stuck thinking about his sister and why she was able to come in contact with him. It didn't matter, because maybe this would bring her back. And if not, then at least he could get more answers.

About an hour passed, and Hector was getting a nice tan. However, he figured it was time to get something to eat and return to his hotel room. And so he did. Before Hector knew it, time had passed and the sun was beginning to set.

"Back to the hotel," he told himself. "And time to get some answers," he said as he drove back. The valet parked his car and Hector returned to his room. *"157,"* he thought to himself. Must've been the same room. But what are the odds of getting the same room his sister did.

He walked back over to the nail polish stain. It was definitely the same exact nail polish his sister used. Either way, he was going to sneak onto the roof tonight. He had no clue if the roof entrance would be unlocked, however.

It was time for Hector to take a shower. He reached into his nightstand for his soap and washcloth. His hand hit something unusual. He grasped it into his palm. It was firm and rectangular shaped. He pulled it out and looked at it. *A key card.* It had the words, **"Roof Access,"** printed on it. And there was a sticky note on it.

"Find her," it read. There was a name on the bottom that signed, "Kristy, aka. cleaning lady," along with a smiley face drawn out. *"How does she know?"* Hector thought to himself. He hasn't told anyone what he was doing, yet somehow this random girl knew.

Either way, this was his ticket. It was time to find the truth. He had to observe that same spot he saw his sister the night she jumped. Hector slipped the card into his pocket and walked out of the hotel room. The hallway was quiet.

It was eleven at night and most people were probably asleep. He made his way to the stairs and opened the door. The slight hum of the florescent lights was the only sound that could be heard. He began ascending the staircase.

Eventually, he made his way to the final door. No more stairs went up. Above the door read, **"Rooftop,"** and on the door was a sign posted with, *"Authorised personnel only! Unauthorised entry could result in prosecution."* But of course, this wasn't going to stop Hector.

Slowly, he slid the key card across the lock. *Beep.* The latch clicked open. He swung the door open and peeked outside. The strong humid air of nighttime Miami hit him. Hector stepped onto the rooftop, the door slamming behind him.

Chapter NINE

Tall fences surrounded the perimeter of the entire rooftop. It wasn't like this five years ago. If only these fences were here before his sister had decided to jump.

Hector began walking towards the spot he remembered standing when his sister jumped. The brick outcropping with graffiti. That was it. He walked over and stood exactly where he did five years ago. Where he tried talking his sister out of it.

He stood there and glanced down at his watch, exactly as eleven thirty hit. He looked back up to see his sister there at the ledge. The fences were now gone. Hector felt a sense of panic. He was reliving it. But something was.. different.

She turned away from the ledge and looked in Hector's direction. "Sis, I miss you. And you know I'll always love you. No matter what," Hector said with tears running down his cheeks. She smiled at him. "I love you too, brother," she said.

Hector smiled back. "Can you please walk away from the ledge?" he asked kindly. But her expression suddenly changed. She looked afraid now. "What.. what's wrong Emma," he asked her. She raised her hand and pointed past Hector, over his shoulder.

"The.. the red man," she said with a fearful tone. Hector slowly turned his head to look over his shoulder. There it was again, only now more clear than ever.

Hector whipped around rapidly and back pedalled a bit too fast. He fell down backwards onto his behind. Charred dark red skin. Eyes pitch black with no soul. Legs that faded into nothingness and that notorious red glow that he remembered.

It began walking towards him, grunting loudly and angrily. The sound of those bells again. *Ding. Ding. Ding.* Each step he took, he only sounded angrier. Hector knew he had to do something.

He threw himself back up onto his feet and began running towards the roof's exit door, but something stopped him. A pulling force, one he could not resist. As if something was wrapped around his waist, pulling him back, only nothing was physically there.

Hector kept trying to fight it, planting his foot out like an anchor. It wasn't working. He was slowly sliding across the concrete towards the red man. He looked up at the red man, who was getting closer. A grimacing smile appeared on his face. No teeth, just like he saw on that girl. There was no hair either, exposing his charred and torn up scalp.

His sister screamed something at Hector. "Look at me!" she said. He turned his head toward his sister, still getting pulled. "You need to look him in the eyes," she explained. "And tell him this," she continued.

A serious expression formed onto her face. *"Release your soul into hell and lock yourself away. Rid of the torment you've brought her and escape where you belong,"* she said with rhythm.

Hector paused for a moment, then looked the horrifying creature in it's black empty eyes. *"Release your soul into hell and lock yourself away,"* he paused, trying to remember. The red man was now only ten feet from him.

His sister began to speak, only this time, it was in Hector's own mind. As if she spoke through his thoughts and now he knew what to say.

"Rid of the torment you've brought her," he continued out loud with confidence. *"And escape where you belong."* There was a moment of silence.

The pulling suddenly stopped and Hector was free from the grasp. He stared at the red man as it suddenly burst into flames. A deep and agonising scream could be heard coming from the thing. It's flesh began to melt away, exposing nothing but bone.

Suddenly, a gun shot rang out. The red man dropped in an instant, with a bullet hole between his eyes. He lied there for a moment on the ground, face down and lifeless.

Hector looked back over at his sister, but she was gone again. He whipped his head back towards the corpse, only to see that it was now different. It was a normal looking man now, with black hair and an exit wound on the back of his head.

His body was now covered with a stained white sheet, with just the head exposed. Hector slowly made his way towards the body. Flies circled around the wound, eating away at it's flesh.

He got within arms reach of the body. Hector slowly reached out and pulled away the sheet. There lied a somewhat slim looking individual with a black t-shirt and blue jeans. *"Who is this?"* He thought to himself.

Hector was incredibly curious, so he grabbed the dead man's head and slowly turned it to the side. He still didn't look familiar. Like some stranger was just shot in the back of the head for no reason.

But what did it mean? Why would his sister make him kill a stranger? And what did she mean by, *"Rid of the torment you've brought her."* Something was off. What didn't he know about her death?

A beep sounded from the locked rooftop door and it swung open rapidly. A bunch of men with rifles stormed out and began shouting at Hector. "On the ground!" one of them shouted. He complied, not wanting to get shot.

"Place your hands on your head and don't move!" the man shouted. Hector did as he was told. The armed men moved towards him and violently pulled his hands down behind his back, locking Hector into handcuffs.

Chapter TEN

Hector sat in the back of a police car, with the front windows barely cracked open. He could just barely make out what the officers were saying.

"We need to investigate the footage. All I know, is that we were called here because multiple witnesses reported hearing a gunshot from that roof," one of them said, pointing up. "He was the only one up there, I don't see who else could've done it," the officer said.

The conversation was very one sided from Hector's perspective. He could only make out the voice of one officer. "Yeah, the man is obviously deceased. We need to get an autopsy done to find out trajectory and whatnot. For all we know, it could've been a sniper from another roof," the officer continued.

"Right now, we have no hard evidence against him, but he's gotta stay in our custody until we figure this out. Just to be safe." Minutes passed by as Hector still sat in the back of the cop car, handcuffs digging into his skin.

After about an hour or so, one of the officers walked over to Hector's door and opened it. "Hey, so we just reviewed the CCTV footage from that rooftop and we saw you with what looked like a nine millimeter handgun, firing at that man," he explained.

Hector was confused and furious. He did not do such a thing. "What are you talking about?!" he said with frustration. "I did not shoot any-" he explained, but the officer cut him off.

"So at this time, you have the right to remain silent. Anything you do or say can and will be used against you in the court of law. You have the right to an attorney. If you cannot afford one, one will be appointed to you by the state of Florida. Do you understand these rights I have read to you sir?" the officer asked.

"But, I didn't do anything?!" Hector exclaimed. "Sir, we have video evidence of you shooting this man. You cannot tell me you didn't do anything," the officer replied. "Well, can you show me then?" Hector asked. "We've pulled the tapes. We'll show you as soon as we get to the station," the officer explained.

They both sat there for a moment in silence. "Sit tight bud," the officer said to him as he shut the car door.

Hector was then driven down to the station. The officer walked him inside, with a flash drive in his hand. They walked into a small office with a computer. The officer stuck the flash drive into the computer and waited.

A video popped up on the screen. It was the rooftop. There must've been a camera hidden somewhere by the exit. The officer scrubbed through the footage until he found the clip he needed.

On the footage, Hector opened the door to the rooftop and made his way over to the spot, just like he remembered. However, his sister was not there. But that man was, and he looked like he did when Hector saw him lying there. No *red man* or anything. Just a normal looking human being.

The video then showed Hector reaching into his waistband and pulling out a pistol. Just seconds later, a flash and the man dropped. "See," the officer said pointing at the screen. "That's why you're in handcuffs right now."

It didn't make any sense. How was this even possible. He didn't shoot anybody. He didn't even have a weapon on him. All he did was say some words to save himself and his sister, but the footage showed otherwise.

"I'm being completely serious officer, I really didn't do that. I recall seeing my sister up there. There was a red man trying to attack us, so I said a few things that my sister told me, and he lit up in flames and dropped," Hector explained to the officer.

But the officer just looked at him like he was crazy. "Alright, that's enough," he said, grabbing Hector by the arm. "You're just trying to mess with me now," the officer said as they walked over to get him booked.

After a while, Hector was finally placed into a holding cell. He was going to have to try to fight this at court. They were just going to think he was schizophrenic or something, seeing things that weren't there.

Hector began crying. *"What is happening?"* he thought to himself *"Am I actually just losing it?"* But as soon as that thought crossed his mind, a voice responded to him. "No, you're not losing it Hector," a familiar voice called out. He looked up. It was his sister again, standing on the other side of the bars.

He stood up in his cell and walked over to her. "You've gotta get me outta this, I'm innocent!" Hector said through his tears. She reached her hand through the bars and held something out. *A screwdriver.*

Hector grabbed it from her hands. "What do I do with this?" he asked. She looked up at the ceiling behind him. "The vent," she explained. "It leads you to the public restrooms at the front of the building."

He looked at the vent. Four screws held the cover in place. It looked very tight, but Hector was going to have to really squeeze himself through. He turned back towards his sister. "Get to the bathrooms and I'll help you from there," she said with a smile. Hector smiled back. "Thank you," he said.

She then turned around and disappeared into the darkness of the hallway. He looked down at the screwdriver in his hand and sighed. "Time to get out of here," he thought to himself.

Just as the thought crossed his mind, a shadow flashed across the room and a door creaked open. "Need something to eat kid?" a voice called out. It was the sheriff. Hector quickly ran over to his bed and slipped the screwdriver under the mattress. "I think I'm good for now," he yelled back.

The sheriff rounded the corner and stared at Hector through the bars, hands crossed behind his back. The man was a giant. He had to be at least be six foot four, while Hector stood there at only five foot ten. The sheriff stood there for a moment, staring with cold eyes.

"Stay put," he said. "Do you really think I can go anywhere anyway?" Hector replied with confusion, trying to act it out the best he could. The sheriff rolled his eyes and walked away, closing the door behind him.

Hector instantly ran back over to the

mattress and grabbed the screwdriver. *"I won't go to jail,"* he thought to himself as he pulled a metal chair over from the corner of his cell. *"Not for something I didn't do,"* he continued in his head.

He placed the chair directly beneath the vent and stood up onto it. Hector began turning each screw, one by one. Eventually, the vent cover popped loose. He slowly removed it and walked back over to his mattress, shoving it underneath.

Hector then stepped back onto the chair and looked up. It was dark, so he was going to have to feel his way through. He reached up and felt around. There was a bend in the vent where it turned horizontal. He was going to have to grab the ledge and pull himself inside.

With as much strength as possible, Hector pulled himself up. It was a tight squeeze, but there was at least some breathing room. He began shimmying his way through the ventilation shaft.

After about five minutes of inching himself forward, Hector stumbled across another vent cover directly beneath him. It was pitch black beneath but it had to be the bathroom.

The scent of cleaner mixed with urine plunged into his nostrils. *"Yep, that's definitely the bathroom,"* he thought to himself. But how was he supposed to move the vent cover?

Hector took a deep breath, raised his elbow and slammed down on the cover as hard as he could. To his surprise, it dropped to floor. *Clank!* The sound of metal hitting concrete echoed into the darkness.

Hopefully it would not draw the sheriff attention, if he was still in the building. Hector slowly made his way down the dark opening, not know how far of a drop it was. *"One, two.. three,"* Hector counted in his head as he dropped into the darkness.

Chapter ELEVEN

He landed safely onto the smooth concrete floor. It was pitch black, but Hector could barely make out some light peering underneath a closed door. He carefully made his way over and felt around for a switch. *Flick.* The room filled with light.

It took a moment for his eyes to adjust, but Hector eventually spotted something in the corner of the bathroom, next to the sink. It was his sister. She was here, just like she promised.

She smiled at Hector. "I told you I'd be here," she said. He smiled back. "You were always there for me Em," Hector said. His expression then changed. "But, I wasn't there for you," he said. There was a moment of silence.

Emma walked over to Hector and placed a hand on his shoulder. "Don't say that Hector," she said with a look of forgiveness. "Sometimes, we don't realise how much we're actually worth in someone else's life," she continued. "Why else would I be talking to you right now?"

A tear rolled down Hector's cheek. He looked back up at his sister and nodded. "Lead the way," he said. Emma reached out and grabbed Hector by the hand, leading him to the far end of the bathroom.

She then let go and placed both her hands against the wall. Emma looked over at Hector and gestured towards the wall with her head. "Place your hands like this," she explained.

He placed his hands against the wall, just like Emma. A tingling sensation trickled through his fingertips and down his body. In an instant, the wall crumbled to pieces. Hector jumped back in shock. "What the hell?" he said.

Emma looked over at him and smiled. "Don't worry about it," she said. "Told you I was getting you out of this mess." They both turned back towards the hole in the wall, as the wind from outside whipped through their hair.

Emma gestured forward. "You first," she said. Hector slowly stepped past the debris and into the outside world. But something was different. It was scorching hot and he was surrounded by nothing but sand. He was in a desert.

He looked back at where the hole in the wall was. It was gone. His sister stood there with a smile and pointed ahead of Hector. There was a long winding and what looked to be never ending trail dug into the sand. "We need to follow this," she said.

Hector was confused. How did he end up in a desert? And what was at the end of this trail? There was only one way to find out. He started walking down the path with Emma directly behind. She stopped him for a moment.

"You'll need this," she said, holding out a large bottle of water. "Thanks," Hector replied. He began walking again. "Wait," she said, stopping him again. He turned around. Emma was holding something in her right hand. She held her hand out, opening up her fingers to reveal a shiny brass key.

Hector paused for a moment and looked up at her. "What's this for?" he asked. But she didn't respond. "Just take it, please," she said. Hector nodded and took the key from her hand, then continued walking down the path.

It felt like a hundred degrees and Hector was sweating bullets. His water was running out fast. "How much farther," he asked Emma. "We're almost there," she replied. Hector sighed and nodded. "Alright," he replied.

After lots of walking, something did eventually appear ahead on the path. It was a large temple of some sort. Two large doors that stood at roughly ten feet tall with sandy stone walls surrounding it. It took a while to finally reach the doors, but once they did, Emma walked out in front.

"Let's go inside," she said, pushing one of the extremely heavy looking doors wide open. Hector walked in with his sister as the loud menacing stone door slammed behind them.

The entire inside of the temple was lit with torches, burning infinitely. The walls on the inside looked ancient. In the center of the temple was a fancy looking storage chest. Emma walked out in front and gestured at

Hector.

"Come on," she said, leading the way. They walked forward slowly, till they eventually reached the chest. A rusted old lock held it closed. Emma pointed at the chest. "The key," she said. "Open it." He reached into his pocket and pulled out the key.

Slowly, Hector walked towards the chest. He crouched down and inserted the key into the lock. *Click.* The chest was now unlocked. He looked back at Emma for a second, who was grinning wide with joy. She gestured at the chest again.

Hector turned back towards the chest and took a deep breath. The chest creaked open slowly as he lifted the lid. Inside was a blue marble ball about four inches in diameter.

It glowed with a faint white light, like it was living. Hector reached out slowly with both hands and picked it up. On contact, he felt an electric-like sensation in his fingertips. He turned towards his sister, who was now crying.

"Bring it here," she said with tears in her

eyes. Hector slowly walked over to her. As they were both just inches from each other, Emma reached out with both hands, grasping the marble ball.

The electrical sensation was now stronger than ever, coursing through Hector's veins. He felt a connection like never before now with his sister. The ball glowed brighter than ever, shooting white rays of light everywhere.

Suddenly, the ball melted away in their hands and was no longer a solid object, but a bundle of electricity and light. They both looked each other in the eyes. Sending signals back and forth that neither one could control. Another force entered the room. They both looked over to see what it was.

Chapter TWELVE

It was the girl from before. All white eyes, an empty smiling mouth and a missing nose with a scar across the face. *"It must be an alternate version of his sister,"* Hector thought to himself.

The girl began walking towards them. "We have to expel her as well," Emma said, releasing her grip from the ball of energy. As soon as she did, the electrical sensations stopped and the connection with his sister was interrupted. However the ball stayed in Hector's hands.

Emma started walking towards the other girl. They were the exact same height and everything. Only, one was completely evil and full of hatred while the other was the truly joyful sister that he knew and loved.

Emma started speaking to the other girl, in a language he had never heard before. The other girl replied back in a harsh and hateful tone of voice that did not sound human. It sounded like they were arguing, but Hector had no clue what they were saying.

They eventually were face to face screaming at each other. The evil girl pushed Emma to the ground then stuck both her hands out. Emma started screaming out in pain as she lifted feet first off the ground.

"Stop!" Hector screamed out with fear. Tears started running down his face. He needed to do something. Hector looked over at the ball of energy in his hands. He thought deeply of his sister and how much he missed her after she passed.

All of the emotions flowed through him and the ball of energy split between his fingertips, running down his arms and into his heart. The energy was now part of him. Hector turned and began walking towards the struggle.

The evil girl looked at Hector with anger and confusion. She then released Emma from her grasp, dropping her onto her face. The evil girl then raised her hands at Hector in an attempt to control him, but it did not work.

He was far too powerful now. The evil girl stood there in shock. Hector stuck his right fist into the air, sending a brutal shock wave into the girl's direction. She flew backwards onto her back.

Emma ran over and stood behind Hector in fear. The evil girl lied there for a moment, dazed. Hector then turned around to face Emma. He reached his hands out and gripped onto her shoulders, sending energy towards her.

Something formed behind Emma. It was a large figure of a lion standing at about twenty feet tall, made solely out of that same blue energy that Hector had harnessed. They both seemed to be able to control its movements with their minds as long as they worked together.

Hector looked at Emma and nodded. They both stepped out of the way to let the beast through. It roared, shaking the entire temple. The evil girl sat there, struck with fear. The lion then charged at her, pinning her down. Then, it got really violent.

Emma and Hector no longer had control

over the beast. It began ripping the girl apart, piece by piece. The demonic screaming of the woman echoed throughout the temple. It was too violent for both Hector and Emma to watch.

Eventually, the lion finished it's job. It then turned towards Emma and Hector, blood still dripping from it's mouth. It formed a slight human-like smirk and turned towards the back wall of the temple. It primed itself up and charged, crashing through the wall and running off into the emptiness of the desert.

Both Emma and Hector sat there for a moment in awe. An interference scrambled through Hector's mind. Like some sort of static. His ears began ringing.

Hector clutched the sides of his head, grunting in pain. Then, it stopped. A sense of relief flushed over him. Something changed. Hector felt suddenly free for some reason.

"Was it over now?" Hector thought to himself. A voice replied in his head. *"Yes brother, it is,"* Emma's voice rang out in his head. They both turned and smiled at each other. In an instant, the environment around them suddenly shifted. They both looked

around.

They were surrounded by palm trees and sand, with the ocean's waves crashing against the shore. Directly across from them was a beach-side gift shop named, "Rafael's Fine Souvenirs." It was the last place they hung out right before his sister took her life.

Was he back in the past again? Did he reverse time somehow? Emma stood there, tears forming on her face. Hector looked down at his watch. *August 5th, 2019.* The exact date his sister passed. Only now, they had the knowledge of what was supposed to happen tonight.

Hector looked at his sister with tears in his eyes and said three words, "Don't do it." A slight smile formed on her face through the tears. She walked towards Hector and gave him a big hug. "I won't," she said not letting go. "You've rid of my demons. I feel.. alright again," she said through a smile and tears.

The End.

Thanks for reading!

Summary

A young man named Hector is just getting by with life. He works his nine to five everyday, just barely getting by. Not to mention, trouble seems to follow him wherever he goes. But something strange happens one night and he cannot unsee it.

He witnesses a young girl take her life from the rooftop of his workplace. However, no true evidence could be discovered to tell that anything actually happened. Was it real? Or was he just seeing things?

The next few days, Hector is hit with many more paranormal encounters relating to the event. Now, he must find answers. He returns to the same rooftop one night to look for any clues. However, somebody called the police on him and Hector does not want to get caught for trespassing, so he attempts to run from the police.

As he does, he gets swept down stream in a violent current. Hanging from a branch now, Hector sees the same girl from the other night. Except this time, he is able to see her face, and it is something truly demonic.

Hector escapes from the grasp of the branch only to be chased by something else ten times for terrifying. He finds himself hiding in a public restroom from this monster. He then manages to outsmart it and escape back into the woods, only to be met with the evil girl. However, something about her has now changed.

The face of his sister that he lost five years ago due to a suicide incident. He wakes up in a hospital after falling unconscious and remembers everything that happened. Now, he must find answers. Could he really get his sister back?

As the days go on, Hector is given more clues by the spirit of his sister. He must go to the Charles Dahlman hotel in Miami, where his sister took her life. Hector drives out there and stays for a night. The room service lady he met somehow knows about Hector's sister and slips him a roof access key card.

Hector takes the opportunity and makes his way onto the roof, where everything happened five years ago with his sister. It all unfolds again and the same monster that chased him a couple nights ago is back. However, his sister instructs Hector on how to eliminate him. And so he listens.

He now gets framed for murder, as the monster he killed ended up being an innocent man, which Hector did not actually shoot. He is placed in a holding cell by the sheriff's department where he sees his sister again.

She helps him escape, but leads him somewhere else, where all the answers are held. A stone temple in the middle of the desert. They unlock a chest to find a marble ball of energy. It all unfolds now. Hector and his sister both grab this marble ball only to connect them together once again.

However, someone else has shown up to ruin it all. The evil girl Hector seen before, only now she's here for a fight. Hector ends up saving his sister's life through their bond of energy, by releasing a beast to put an end to the evil girl.

They are now freed. Hector looks up to find himself on the beach with his sister on the same night and year she took her life. She promises not to do it again and Hector now has his sister back that he missed so much.

Special Thanks To:

You, the reader.

And of course my friends and family who all play a role in my future and success. Those beautiful people are:

Tammy, David, Shea, Alexavier, Hollie, Tom, Kendyl, Tim, Debbie, Darlene, Carol, Dana, Kevin, Marc, Alexander, Seth, Bryan and Ryan.

About the Author

Hello, I am Jonathan A. Miller. I was born on the year of 2002 in Scranton, Pennsylvania. I am somewhat of a new author, as this is my second book. When I am creating, I make sure to always write from the heart and put one hundred percent into it. In case you wanted to know some of my personal hobbies, I love to write, lift weights, go to the beach and dance at clubs. One of my favourite quotes has to be:

"A new day, you can go, you can do anything you wanna. It's your play, swing low, go high anywhere you wanna. You can reach for the moon, anywhere your dreams could take you."

From the song, "Yesterday," by Imagine Dragons, my favourite band of all time. It's your life, do whatever you want with it. Don't let anyone tell you otherwise. You're the master of your sea.

Copyright © 2024 by Jonathan A. Miller

All rights reserved.

No part of this publication may be reproduced, distributed, or transmitted in any form or by any means, including photocopying, recording, or other electronic or mechanical methods, without the prior written permission of the publisher, except as permitted by U.S. copyright law. For permission requests, contact (607)398-1323.

The story, all names, characters, and incidents portrayed in this production are fictitious. No identification with actual persons (living or deceased), places, buildings, and products is intended or should be inferred.

Book Cover by Jonathan A. Miller

www.ingramcontent.com/pod-product-compliance
Lightning Source LLC
Chambersburg PA
CBHW051806130726
47987CB00003B/1129